# THE ADVENTURES OF "CHUCK E. BEAVER" AND FRIENDS

# THE BIG FIGHT

Written by
**Kiki**

Illustrated by
**ROBERT ELLIOTT**

Published by
**Montbec Inc.**

**Publisher**
MATT ARENY

**Publication Advisor**
JOSE AZEVEDO

**Editorial Supervisor**
ETHEL SALTZMAN

**Artwork Supervisor**
PIERRE RENAUD

**ISBN 2-89227-206-8**

# THE BIG FIGHT

It was the start of a very ordinary day for the Beaver household.

Everyone was busy getting ready for work and school. Chuck E. was now into his second month at school and everything was going fine. He had made many new friends and was learning exciting things every day.

Chuck E. arrived at school that day with his best friend Bobby Bear, and as the school bell rang they quickly made their way into the classroom.

While everyone awaited the arrival of Mrs. Groundhog, the teacher, Chuck E. was busy putting his books away in his desk.

Just as everyone had quieted down, Mrs. Groundhog made her way into the classroom.

And coming into the room right behind Mrs. Groundhog was a new student.

"Class, I'd like you all to meet our newest student who will be joining us today," said Mrs. Groundhog. "His name is Wally Wolverine."

While the class was saying hello, Chuck E. was having a good look at his new classmate. He noticed that Wally was much taller and looked stronger than most of the boys in his class.

Chuck E. thought to himself that Wally looked a bit mean and it might be the best thing for Chuck E. to stay out of Wally's way just to be sure.

The only seat that was left in the class for Wally was at the back of Chuck E.'s row. As Wally was making his way to his seat he passed by Chuck E.'s desk. Unfortunately, Chuck E. had left his foot in the aisle, and as Wally passed by, he tripped over it and fell face down on the classroom floor. The whole class burst out laughing at the sight, but Wally was not amused.

Wally picked himself up, his face red with embarrassment, and glared at Chuck E. Chuck E. attempted to apologize but Wally was not forgiving.

"I'll see you later, after school!" Wally whispered harshly to Chuck E.

"B-B-But I-I didn't mean it," Chuck E. tried to explain. Wally wasn't listening as he headed towards his seat. Chuck E. was upset now at the thought of Wally wanting to beat him up. He thought, "It's not right to fight, as Pop always said, because there are far better ways to solve disagreements."

Chuck E. had to think. "How can I avoid a fight with Wally?" he wondered. "If I try to sneak home without him seeing me he'll only catch up with me tomorrow and he'll be even madder!"

Chuck E. was very nervous about what had happened and the thought of what was to come.

It was almost lunch time before Chuck E. realized it. As the bell rang to begin lunch all of the children jumped up and quickly filed out the door. Only Chuck E. and his friend Bobby Bear remained.

"Chuck E., aren't you coming to lunch?" Bobby asked. "I'm n-n-not really hungry today," Chuck E. replied nervously, "y-you go on without me, Bobby. I don't want you to miss any of your lunch."

"Alright, then. I'll see you after lunch," Bobby answered.

As Bobby made his way out of the classroom he bumped into Mrs. Groundhog passing by.

"Oh, excuse me!" Bobby said. "That's okay, Bobby," Mrs. Groundhog replied. "Why are you so late for lunch, Bobby?" she continued. "Well, I was waiting for my friend Chuck E., but he says he doesn't feel like eating today," Bobby explained. "Okay then, go on to your lunch now," Mrs. Groundhog said.

Then Mrs. Groundhog looked into the classroom and saw Chuck E. staring out of the window at the other children eating their lunches.

"Chuck E!" Mrs. Groundhog questioned him, "why aren't you going to lunch today?"

"I-I wanted to catch up on my reading, Mrs. Groundhog," Chuck E. stammered. "Well, I guess that'll be okay for today, but I don't want you to miss your lunch again," Mrs. Groundhog responded. "I won't, Mrs. Groundhog," Chuck E. promised.

"Oh, what am I to do?" Chuck E. thought to himself. "I can't stay in tomorrow, and what's going to happen to me when I try to go home tonight?"

"I'm going to have to face Wally even though he's probably going to beat me up," Chuck E. decided, "but I'm not going to fight with him because it's not right to fight."

"Pop always told me that it is better to talk out your differences with other people than to fight," Chuck E. remembered. "It takes a lot more strength not to fight than to fight, his pop used to say," Chuck E. thought, "and that's what I'm going to do."

Just at that moment the lunch bell rang and soon all of the students began rushing into the classroom to take their seats.

Wally Wolverine came into the classroom and stopped beside Chuck E.'s desk. "I didn't see you at lunch, Chuck E. Chicken," Wally said angrily. "You can't hide forever."

"I don't want to fight with you, Wally!" Chuck E. replied. "It was an accident that you tripped over my foot and I tried to apologize for it."

"I don't care about your apologies," Wally responded. "Everyone laughed at me and you're going to pay for that!"

"Wally, would you kindly take your seat!" Mrs. Groundhog requested. At that Wally hurried to his seat and sat down.

By now, Chuck E. was becoming more and more anxious and upset at the thought of having to face Wally after school. Chuck E.'s friend Bobby Bear had overheard the conversation between Chuck E. and Wally, and tried to console Chuck E. about his fears.

"Chuck E., why does Wally want to fight with you?" Bobby asked.

"He thinks that because everyone laughed at him for falling they think he's stupid and clumsy," Chuck E. explained. "I guess we wouldn't have liked it if all the kids laughed at us on our first day here."

"Are you going to fight him, Chuck E?" Bobby continued.

"No, I'm not going to fight him!" Chuck E. replied.

"I think he's just trying to prove that he's strong so people won't laugh at him, so I'm going to try to be his friend."

"I sure hope you're right, Chuck E.," Bobby said, "because I wouldn't want to see you beat up."

The afternoon went by even more quickly than the morning and Chuck E. spent most of it staring at the school clock hoping that the day wouldn't end. But of course it did, and as the clock struck 3:30 the school bell rang loudly.

While the other children were rushing to collect their books and coats and leave for home, Chuck E. was purposely taking a lot of time to get ready.

Everyone had left the classroom by now except for Chuck E. and Bobby.

"Say, Chuck E!" Bobby suggested, "maybe Wally forgot about the fight and left for home already!"

"Maybe you're right, Bobby!" Chuck E. responded hopefully. "Why don't we head for home now. I don't see Wally outside anywhere."

As Chuck E. and Bobby headed towards the school bus, Wally suddenly appeared right in front of Chuck E.

"Where do you think you're going, CHICKEN E?" Wally questioned.

"I-I-I'm going home," Chuck E. responded.

"Oh, no you're not, not before I settle the score for what you did to me today!" Wally said angrily.

"B-B-But Wally, I don't want to fight with you. The kids weren't laughing at you, they were laughing only because of what happened," Chuck E. tried to explain.

"I don't care!" Wally cried out. "People won't laugh at me anymore when they know how strong I am, after I beat you up!"

By this time, there was a crowd surrounding both Chuck E. and Wally, anxiously anticipating a fight.

"I-If you feel that you have to beat me up to show how strong you are then go ahead," Chuck E. replied, "b-b-but I'm not going to fight with you because I want to be your friend."

"You want to be my friend?" Wally asked. "Why would you want to be my friend, when I'm going to beat you up."

"W-Well, first of all I don't really believe that you want to beat me up," Chuck E. answered, "and, secondly, you're new here and I just want to show you that we are really friendly and we would like the chance to get to know you."

"R-Really! That's great!" said Wally with surprise. "I really didn't want to fight with you but I don't like being laughed at," Wally explained. "I felt because people were laughing at me that they didn't want to be my friends," he continued.

"Of course we do!" everyone shouted.

"Wow! That's fantastic!" Wally beamed.
"I'm sure glad I didn't have to fight to
make friends. I-I-I really don't like to
fight, you know."

"You're not half as glad as I am,"
Chuck E. said with relief. "I was wondering
how I was going to explain to my pop
how I got a black eye at school today."

"Say, Wally, why don't you come over
to my house and we can play together!"
Chuck E. asked.

"Okay, Chuck E !" Wally replied, "but
first I have to go home and ask my mom."

"That's fine with me," Chuck E. replied. "You know, I think we're going to be great friends. We just got off on the wrong foot if you know what I mean!" Chuck E. laughed.

And with that the rest of the crowd, including Wally, started laughing, feeling happy and relieved.

That evening Wally and Chuck E. played together and had lots of fun, enjoying each other's company. It was the beginning of a long and happy friendship.

It's not right to fight to prove one's might.

Just extend a hand and let friendship stand.

Your friend,

Chuck E.

PRINT IN U.S.A.